The Man
Who Entered
a Contest

The Man Who Entered a Contest

by *Phyllis Krasilovsky*
illustrated by *Yuri Salzman*

Doubleday & Company, Inc., Garden City, New York

In memory of Celia Liniow,

the best baker I ever knew

E

KRA

Library of Congress Catalog Card Number 79-3112

ISBN 0-385-13351-0 Trade
ISBN 0-385-13352-9 Prebound
Text copyright © 1980 by Phyllis Krasilovsky
Illustrations copyright © 1980 by Yuri Salzman
All Rights Reserved
Printed in the United States of America

9 8 7 6 5 4 3 2

There was once a man

who lived with his cat

in a little house

on the edge of a town.

Every night, he cooked himself

a big, big supper.

He liked to cook,

but most of all

he liked to bake cakes.

Every Saturday,

the man would bake one.

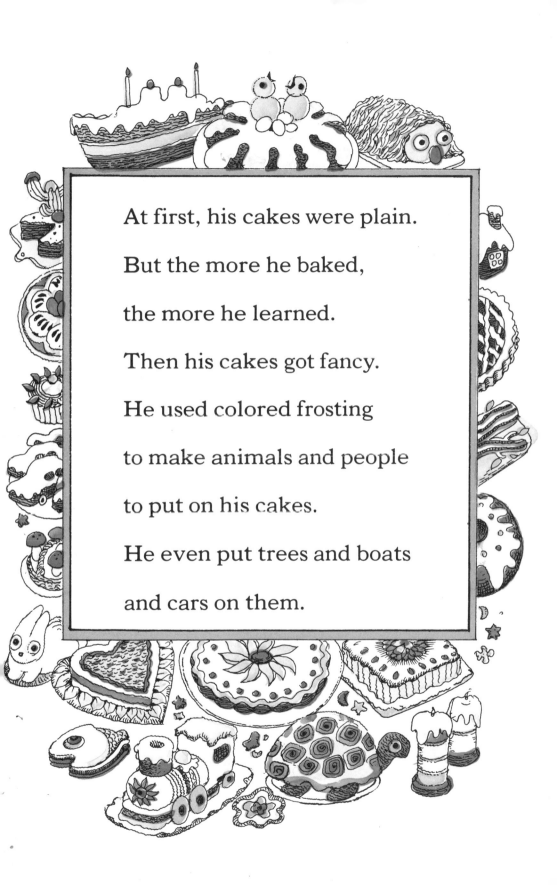

At first, his cakes were plain.

But the more he baked,

the more he learned.

Then his cakes got fancy.

He used colored frosting

to make animals and people

to put on his cakes.

He even put trees and boats

and cars on them.

The man's cat liked

to sit on the table

and watch him work.

But he had to put her up

on the shelf because she liked

to lick the frosting!

One day, the oven

in his old stove

broke down.

No matter how he tried,

the man could not fix it.

The repair man came from town

and fixed it for him.

But he told the man

that the oven would work

only one more time.

Then it would stop working

for good.

"That stove is so old,"

the repair man said.

"You should throw it away."

But the man did not have

enough money

to buy a new one.

He could still cook things

on top of the stove.

But he was not happy.

He missed the fun

of baking a cake

on Saturday.

He knew he could use the oven

one more time.

"Maybe I will bake one last cake

when my birthday comes,"

he thought sadly.

One evening,

the man sat down

to read his newspaper.

He read about

a cake-baking contest.

It would be held on Saturday.

Three judges would pick

the best cake.

The baker would win

a brand-new stove!

This was just what

the man needed!

So he entered the contest.

He sent his address to the judges.

They could come on Saturday

to see what he had baked.

The next night,

the man polished

his big wooden table.

He took out all

his mixing bowls.

He took out all

his mixing spoons.

He took out cups and pans.

The man cleaned

his poor old stove.

He made it shine.

Then he sat down

to read his cookbooks.

He wanted to find

the best recipe.

He read and read.

None of the recipes

looked just right.

"Why don't I make

my own recipe?"

the man thought.

"Then my cake

will be the best.

And it will be different

from any other cake!"

So he decided

to make a giant cake.

He would make flowers

out of frosting.

He would put them

all over the cake.

It would be a garden cake.

The next day, the man

went to the store.

He bought a giant

bag of flour.

The flour would

make the cake rich.

He bought a giant

bag of sugar.

The sugar would

make the cake sweet.

He bought a tall can

of baking powder.

Baking powder works like magic

to make cakes rise.

It makes a cake

lighter and higher.

The man bought

a big bottle of vanilla.

The vanilla would give

the cake flavor.

He bought a box of salt.

He bought powdered sugar

for the frosting.

And he bought coloring

to make the cake pretty.

Then he drove to see

a farmer he knew.

He got the biggest eggs.

He got the richest milk.

He got the freshest butter.

His cake would be delicious!

The next day was Saturday.

The man wanted to

get up early.

He set his alarm

for five o'clock

in the morning.

When the alarm rang,

the man jumped up.

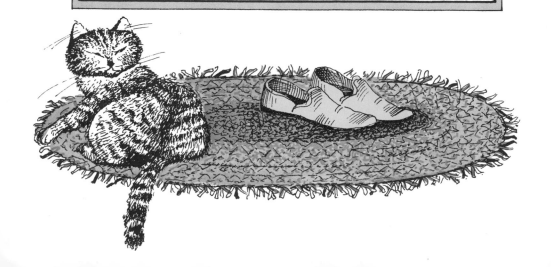

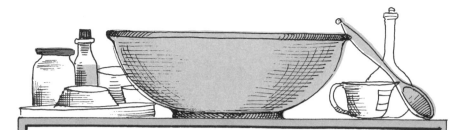

He washed.

He dressed.

He put on his

snow-white apron.

He put on his

snow-white hat.

He ran into the kitchen

to light the oven.

Then he picked out

his biggest bowl.

He put in butter and sugar.

He put in flour and eggs.

He put in milk and vanilla.

He put in salt.

And he put in baking powder

to make the cake rise.

There was a lot of batter

in the bowl.

It was hard work

to mix the batter.

The man got very tired.

He sat down to rest.

He listened to music.

Then he leaned back

and closed his eyes.

While he was resting,

his cat jumped

off the shelf.

She knocked over

the can of baking powder.

More baking powder

went into the bowl!

The man did not know

what the cat had done.

When the man got up,

he mixed the batter again.

He poured it

into the pans.

He put the pans

into the oven.

Then he started

to clean the house.

He wanted it

to look nice

for the judges.

He went out to

sweep.

He was very busy.

He did not see

what was happening

in his kitchen.

The cakes were rising.

Because of the extra baking powder,

they were rising too much.

They were growing

RIGHT OUT OF THE OVEN DOOR!

They were covering

EVERYTHING IN SIGHT!

The batter covered

the table.

Now there was

a table cake!

The batter covered

the chairs.

Now there were

chair cakes!

There was a

mixing-bowl cake.

There were spoon cakes.

There were curtain cakes.

There was a sink cake.

There was a

dish-towel cake.

There was a

rocking-chair cake.

There were

flower-pot cakes.

There was even a

garbage-can cake.

But the biggest cake of all

was the STOVE CAKE!

The man finished

sweeping.

He went inside to

clean up the kitchen.

What a sight!

The man was as surprised

as he could be!

He stared at

all the kitchen cakes.

He almost sat down in

the rocking-chair cake!

He did not know what to do.

He did not have time

to clean up the cakes

before the judges came.

And even if he did clean them up,

he would not have a cake

for the contest.

The man felt awful.

"Oh dear," he groaned.

Just then, the judges came in.

"We came a little early,"

the first judge said.

He looked into the kitchen.

"My goodness!" he said.

"What is this?"

"A whole kitchen of cake!"

said the second judge.

"It is so big,"

said the third judge,

"and so different.

Just look at the stove cake!"

"This is wonderful!"

the judges said all together.

They gave the man

the prize right away.

The man was so happy!

he asked everyone from town

to help eat the cakes.

They had a party.

They ate the curtain cakes.

They ate the sink cake.

They ate the flower-pot cakes.

They ate *all* the cakes—

even the stove cake.

Everyone thought the cakes

were just delicious.

That afternoon, the

brand-new stove came.

It was white and shining.

It had **TWO** big ovens.

It had glass doors.

The man could look inside.

He could see

his cakes rising.

The stove even

had a timer.

A bell rang when

the cakes were ready.

The man sat in

his rocking chair.

He looked and looked

at the new stove.

His cat sat

on his lap.

She purred happily.

She wondered what

all the fuss

had been about!

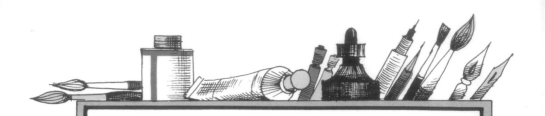

PHYLLIS KRASILOVSKY is well known for her wonderful stories for children, among which are *The Cow Who Fell in the Canal* and *The Man Who Didn't Wash His Dishes.* Her first Reading-On-My-Own book was *The Man Who Tried to Save Time.*

Ms. Krasilovsky and her husband live in Chappaqua, New York, and are the parents of four children. The author often travels to other countries on writing assignments, but when she is in the United States she frequently speaks at schools and libraries.

YURI SALZMAN is an award-winning illustrator and writer of children's books who was born in Moscow. Before emigrating from the USSR in 1976, Mr. Salzman illustrated about ninety children's books, with examples of his work being exhibited officially in the Soviet Union and other countries.

Mr. Salzman now lives in New York State with his wife, Mariana, who is a concert pianist, and their teenage son, Alexander.